Missing

A Suspense-filled Mystery for

Young Readers

By Makenzie R. Casseday

PAVE PRESS 81-2447736, 408 W. Maple St., Dallastown, PA 17313
pavepress1@gmail.com

P. A. V. E. PRESS

ISBN: 978-1-7334590-4-4

LCCN: 9781733459044

Cover Design: PixelStudio

May 2020

TABLE OF CONTENTS

Chapter 1

Once upon a time there was a princess, well I think I am because I'm rich. I'm Lola and this is my story. I'm 13 years old and I love to go outside and feel the fresh warm air with the sweet smell of roses from my family's garden. I love flowers, especially red roses, which are my favorite. My older sister, Bonnie, loves sunflowers because she tells me they're different than any other flower.

Bonnie has a little wild side, the kind of girl that loves to go to parties or clubs with her friends. Bonnie is 18 and loves the rich lifestyle. Me, on the other hand, I don't like the feeling of being wealthy. I just want to be a regular kid and go to a regular school, but instead, I must attend a private school with all the other wealthy kids. I would love to leave the house whenever I want, like my sister, but I can't. I'm told I'm not old enough. So for now, I just have to imagine in my mind all the adventures I could have outside this yard.

Bonnie and I were close to our mom, however, she died in a horrible car crash a few years ago. Well, that's what my dad said. After our mother passed away, that's when Bonnie really started acting out. Our dad is one of the best dads in the world, but he recently remarried.

I don't get along with my stepmother, Veronica, very much. We argue all the time. We never see eye to eye. She never listens to me and what I have to say. We have nothing in common! Right now, I just want the impossible. I want my real mom back. Bonnie, on the other hand, loves Veronica. They're best friends and never fight or argue over anything. I go to our family's flower garden, to have some alone time away from Veronica, to think and sort out the thoughts in my head.

This morning, as usual, Veronica leaves to go to work. Her job entails making and designing dresses. Bonnie quite obviously always wants to go along, and probably would, if it weren't for school. This morning, after Veronica leaves, my usual morning routine is interrupted. My journey to the bathroom is held up by Bonnie beating me there. We meet in the bathroom doorway.

Pushing by me she blurts out, "Better luck next time!" Giggling, she prances into the bathroom.

Sometimes I hate her. I just head back into my room and choose my outfit for the day. I pick out a long bright pink dress with white lace at the bottom. Laying the garments on the bed, I pair them with my black high heels and my very special emerald necklace that my mom gave me.

Not long after I've picked out my clothes, I hear my sister sharply yell my name, "Lola, get your butt over here!"

Naturally, I go over to see what she wants. Bonnie, wearing a towel, asks me if dad has left yet.

"Why are you asking me? Why don't you go see for yourself?" This is the first time in a long time that I've taken a stand to her and I'm feeling proud.

All she says in return is, "I don't know, you little twerp, maybe because I'm smarter than you and since Dad's not here, I just want you to be downstairs, so I can do a quick pregnancy test."

Shock is what I feel! *Wow, Dad's going to be mad!* I also wonder who the father is. I am about to ask her some other questions, when Bonnie quickly interrupts my thoughts.

"Please don't tell anyone, especially Dad, until I know the test results," she begs.

"Fine," I snap, marching back into my room.

Not long after, I hear my sister yell again, "Holy Crap!" That one word gives me my answer about the possibility of this pregnancy. The test came out positive.

When Bonnie comes out of the bathroom, fully dressed, I ask, "What's wrong? Are you?"

She looks so mad, sad and worried all at the same time. I've never seen her look like that before. She just tells me in a calm voice not to tell Dad until she can find a way herself to explain, and of course, I understand.

After I finish getting dressed it is time for breakfast. We lost track of time because of the whole pregnancy scare. So, my usual breakfast of eggs and toast becomes boring cereal- Apple Jacks.   Before we know it, we quickly have to leave for school. I swiftly grab my bookbag and rush out the door. On my walk to school I think about Bonnie and for the first time in my life, I feel bad for her. *Is Dad going to be mad? And what would Mom have thought about this situation?*

Chapter 2

At school, my best friend, Sophia, is waiting for me. "Hey girl, what's up?"

I really, really want to tell her about Bonnie, but I can't. Bonnie asked me not to tell anyone. I intend to keep that promise, at least for right now.

I just reply, "Nothing much."

When we walk into the classroom, the teacher is writing something on the board. I sit in my usual seat right next to my other friend, Ben. The teacher is talking, but it is hard to pay attention because of my enemy, the mean girl in class, Sharpae. She's been picking on me all year. In one swift throw I receive a crumpled-up piece of paper, which lands perfectly on the top of my desk. Secretly, quickly and quietly I unfold the piece of paper and read what is on it. I see a hand drawn picture of a person that was supposed to be me I'm guessing, saying, "A nerd like you shouldn't have friends!" My hatred for her just gets stronger.

I don't have time to deal with her bull crap anymore. Right then and there, I turn around and give her an evil grin. Not knowing what I have in mind, all she does is smile back and laugh. Just then, I do what anyone else would do and raise my hand so the teacher will call on me.

He asks, "Do you know the answer to question number five?"

I answer, "Ummm, no? But, I have this piece of paper that Sharpae gave me."

The teacher has a surprised look on his face and comes up to me and takes it. He doesn't read it out loud like he usually does, instead he tells Sharpae sternly to go out in the hallway! Right now!

She goes out, but on her way, she sticks out her tongue at me. Soon, the teacher joins her, and the remaining classroom students start to talk amongst one another - chat, gossip, whatever. I try to hear what's going on in the hallway. Straining my ears, all I hear is Sharpae "fake" crying. She does that every time she doesn't get her way.

It isn't long until the teacher and Sharpae come right back into the classroom. The teacher starts talking about school crap again that I don't understand, unable to concentrate.

At the bell, it is lunchtime, chicken fingers that taste like they are stale and a small salad that is mostly spinach. The only good thing is the strawberry milk. School lunches are so gross! I have always sat with my friends at lunch, but today I just want to sit alone.

I want to think about my weird, unusual morning with Bonnie and whatever is happening with her. It already seems so long ago, even though it was just this morning. Then my thoughts drift to the that jerk, Sharpae. I really can't eat. I have no appetite. I really wish I could pack, but Veronica always says, "No! You need to eat like everyone else and eat that slop! Why should you be any different?" I hate her so much. She doesn't understand how gross the school food is.

After lunch, I have math with Miss Smith. This teacher is nice, and math is an easy subject for me. The best thing is, I'm in the same class as Sophia. Today in math we are learning about Geometry - shapes and what they are.

This dumb jock in my class, tries to be a class clown, "What are shapes?"

Everyone in the class just laughs except me. Math is my favorite class, my favorite subject, and I want it taken seriously.

The teacher just gives him a dirty look and says, "Now you have more homework, Mr. Donovan."

Most of the class giggles again. I know he was just trying to be funny, but he now seems a little embarrassed. He sits frowning, and his friends have just stopped laughing at him. The teacher goes back to work and so does everyone else.

Through all the events of this morning I had forgotten, until now, that today is a half day of school. After math class it is time to go home. I gather my book bag and collect my things and wait patiently for the bell to ring. Everyone is talking about several different things. One group of girls is talking about makeup, one group of boys about football. Others are talking about what plans they have for the rest of the day. I'm in my own little lonely group, all by myself. I mean, just me and Sophia. We just sit next to each other and just wait, not saying a word. This silence feels weird because she usually talks to me.

Suddenly, the bell rings and everyone runs out of the classroom like a stampede of cattle. Of course, I'm one of the last ones out because I'm not getting trampled! On my way out of the building, I try to find Sophia because we got separated. I go outside to look for her. While I look around, I am thinking about what I will do when I get home. I'm home alone today. Bonnie will get home later. I've been searching, looking around for Sophia, which seems like an hour and Sophia is nowhere around. I just keep thinking, *Surely, she didn't forget about me! This is so unlike her to forget to meet me! I can't believe she left without me.* Eventually, I just head home alone, taking my time, alone in my thoughts, by myself. Thank goodness I don't live that far, that is why I walk every day.

Chapter 3

At home, I check the mail, like I usually do. The mailbox is empty. I think, *That's odd, there's usually something in here. Oh well, maybe the mail is late, and it will come later.* So, I just walk inside the front door. I put my stuff down in the entryway, in front of an antique end table we have right inside the door in my usual bookbag spot. Like usual, I go right up to my room.

As soon as I get there I sit on my bed and text Sophia and ask why she wasn't outside waiting for me after class. She responds right away and says, "Sorry, I forgot I had band practice." She currently plays the flute in the school band. I feel so mad at her because she didn't tell me and left me outside waiting for her.

I just lie down on my bed thinking of something to do. *I know*, I think, *I can water the flowers! That'll change my mood*! Watering the flowers always relaxes me. So, I walk down the staircase and grab the watering can from the kitchen counter, which is already filled with water because I forgot to empty it last time, and I head to the garden. I'm not really paying attention as I walk. There is so much on my mind.

As I enter the garden gate, I suddenly notice all the dead flowers. *What the heck!* My roses, tulips, pansies, daisies, lilies, blue bells, daffodils, all my pretty precious beautiful flowers are brown. *Dead.* Their crinkled crumpled petals falling to the ground. The sunflowers look like a car ran over them and are flat to the ground. In a panic, I don't know what to do. I put the watering can on the ground and dig my phone out of my pocket. To my surprise, there's no reception. I just used it to text Sophia not that long ago, but now it appears to be disconnected.

Thanks a lot, Veronica, for not paying the bill! You dumb jerk! This is what she does, all the time! She thinks I shouldn't use much electronics or my phone. It's her way of keeping me on a very short leash, her way of controlling me. She says I should go outside, enjoy the fresh air and play. *Play with what?* All we have now is a dead flower garden. We don't have a swing set, no tire swing, or even a soccer ball. Victoria doesn't like those things because she thinks they're dumb and would crowd her yard. She says our family is beyond those conventional things. We should have much nicer things than most people.

I get frustrated, because it's not fair. She tells me to go outside, but never Bonnie. Maybe it's because she doesn't like me, I don't know. So I just put my useless phone back in my pocket, pick up the watering can and head back inside. I'm still wondering, *What happened to my beautiful flower garden?*

On my way inside, I happen to see a dark blue car parked in front of my house, but I don't recognize it. *There's no one inside the car,* I think. *I don't know, maybe it's one of Dad's friends?* I just continue to head inside. I open the back-screen door and suddenly I see everything broken, the house destroyed like someone broke in! I'm sure I would've noticed all this mess when I came through the first time, but I swear it wasn't here!

The dining room table is flipped over. The chairs are thrown across the room laying on their sides. In the kitchen, all our nice antique dishes- all broken. Drawers are open, silverware and other utensils all over the floor, like someone was looking for something in them.

The living room unfortunately shows the same destruction. The room is an utter mess! Plus, I notice the TV is gone! Upstairs, my room seems to be okay. Thank goodness I had decided to wear my most prized possession today, just in case – my mother's emerald necklace!

All this mess and I didn't hear anything from outside. I guess I was too involved in weeping and wallowing over my destroyed flower garden. I don't know what to do! I look outside my window, and I see the suspicious car is now gone. *Maybe they left when they heard me come in from outside?* I'm not sure.

I run over to my Dad's room. It looks like the intruders didn't make it to that room either. I had just wanted to double check. I find my dad's safe in his huge walk-in closet. I happen to know the combination; I figured it out years ago. Everything is still in there, that I can tell. Nothing is missing. *Well that's good, at least they didn't take our money and jewelry*, I think. I still don't know what to do. I can't call anyone because of my stupid phone not working. *Stupid Veronica!* Also no one gets home for a while yet. I can't go to our neighbors because we don't have any close by. I guess I just must wait for Bonnie to get home.

I go back downstairs. Maybe I should clean up a bit, so the house isn't such a mess when Bonnie gets here. Plus, it may pass the time. It'll keep my mind busy. So, I start to clean. I flip the dining room table back over, which takes me forever because it's heavy. Then I put the chairs back where they belong. After I fix the dining room and sweep it, it is time to move on to the living room. I put the cushions back onto the sofa. I don't know what to do about the big screen TV, because it's missing. Kitchen time. This room is one of the worst destroyed. *Maybe because it has the most drawers and places to hide things?* I don't know. I close all the cabinets.

Bonnie will be home soon, I think. So, I just stop what I am doing and sit on the sofa and wait and wait.

It feels like forever since I have no TV to watch or time to waste in our garden. I'd still like to know what happened in that garden. *Why would someone do that to such a nice beautiful garden?*

Chapter 4

R ight when I am about to fall asleep, I hear the entryway door open. For once, I really hope it is Bonnie.

It is her! I am so excited and relieved, for the first time ever, that she's home. I run over to her and hug her like I never have before. She looks at me with a startled surprised look on her face. I hadn't even noticed that she was crying, because I was too excited to see her.

As soon as I see her face, I ask her, "What's wrong"?

She just looks at me, smiles at me and says, "Thanks, I needed that!"

I am surprised and wonder what happened.

Before I have a chance to ask, she suddenly starts to blurt out in an unsteady, quivering voice, "My boyfriend broke up with me! I told him I'm pregnant."

I suddenly feel some emotions for her that I've never had toward her before – worry and pity. I'm not sure who he is. I didn't even know she had a boyfriend, but that is so rude! *How can he do that to her? I want to kick his butt right here and now!* I am so mad!

Bonnie starts to cry again and quickly runs up to her room taking two steps at a time. I want to tell her about the robbery. I need to tell her. Even though I don't want to make her more upset, I know it has to be done. I can't keep something like this from her. She'd find out anyway. I follow her upstairs. I can still hear her crying through her closed door. Again, for the second time that day I feel bad for her, and she should feel lucky because I never do.

I knock softly on her closed wooden door. In an unsteady whimper she yells, "Come in."

I go in. I see her lying on her bed crying into her pillow. I go over to her and hug her again. I say, "I have to tell you something."

She rolls over with tears rolling down her cheeks, her red swollen, glossy eyes staring back at me and asks, "What?"

I look deeply in her eyes and I, myself, start to feel the burning sensation in my eyes as I start to tear up. Then I say calmly, "We got robbed! Our TV is gone, and I'm sure other things are missing, too."

She looks at me with a worried look on her face and starts to pick up her phone. "I already tried that, there's no connection."

She just puts down her phone and tells me, "Follow me." She starts to run downstairs and so I quickly follow her. She runs out the door and goes straight to the car yelling toward me, "Get in!"

As I hop in the car, it occurs to me, *Did she forget to lock the door? And where are we going?* There is no time to go back. As she starts to drive, I look over at her. She has an angry but scared expression on her face. I have never seen that look before. We head down the driveway and then to the road.

I stay silent throughout the whole car ride not knowing where we are going. Soon, as Bonnie hurries out of the car, I discover our destination, a police station.

"Get out," she instructs firmly.

I quickly get out. I don't want to make things worse. I follow Bonnie through the police station door. When we get inside it is packed! There are police officers everywhere and people chattering and talking to them, explaining their issues. While we wait for our turn, we stand next to each other. We wait. After a while one officer does walk over and asks us what we need.

Bonnie starts to speak, "Our house just got robbed."

The officer's face isn't one of surprise at all! He just asks what our names are.

"I'm Bonnie Chang and this is Lola Chang, my sister," she says while pointing at me.

He takes us into his private office and asks us a bunch of questions. I have to do most of the answering, because Bonnie had not been home yet. I tell him about how the house was a mess, everything scattered around. I tell him about the dark blue car I saw in our front yard and about my precious flower garden.

After he asks us his questions, which feels like it takes forever, he tells us to stay here at the station. Then, he leaves the room. While he is gone, Bonnie takes out her phone and starts to call Dad. He doesn't answer, but she leaves a voicemail. The phone is working for her, *What the heck?*

It hasn't been long when the officer comes back into the room with a "buddy" officer. The first one asks where our parents are.

"We tried to reach our dad, but he didn't answer his phone," Bonnie says.

The officer just looks at us and then at the other officer. Without another word, they both leave. When I look out of the office window, I see the officers talking, but I can't hear what they are saying. I look back over to Bonnie. She is trying to contact Dad or Veronica again, but neither of them is answering.

I know why Veronica doesn't answer, she always seems to keep her phone off, especially at work so she can "focus on her job with no distractions." I think that's just a bunch of bull crap. I think it's just so she doesn't have to deal with us, or me. I wish I could call Sophia, but my phone still won't work. I hate that.

Suddenly, both officers come back in and we are asked to follow them. So, we do what we are asked and follow them straight to the front door and to the parked police car. They tell us we did nothing wrong, but we should get in. By all means, we get in. *Who wouldn't get into a police car when told?* Then they ask what our address is. Bonnie tells them, and they enter it into the GPS. They start driving and tell us their plans and their names.

The first officer's name is Officer Truman and the other is Officer Kongsberg. They tell us that they're going back to our house to see if they can find fingerprints, evidence, or any clues as to what happened. I think it is a cool idea but Bonnie, on the other hand, doesn't. She is worried about Dad's reaction if they come back, wondering why there are police officers in the house. I am worried too, but I am more excited that we are in a police car. It's a new experience for me.

It is quiet during the ride. It is so quiet you can probably hear a pin drop. I don't like how quiet it is, so I ask one of the police officers if he can put the radio on.

He just says, "No, I'm sorry, we need the radio open, so we can hear if there is something bad out there."

Well that was awkward, I think.

Chapter 5

Finally, we make it home. It looks like we never left, but I still don't see Dad's or Veronica's car.

"If you don't mind, we are going to take a look around," says Officer Kongsberg.

"That's fine," Bonnie says impatiently.

We all walk inside, and they start looking around.

"Are you sure you got robbed?" asks Officer Kongsberg.

"Yeah," I say. "When I came home everything was flipped over and the cabinets were all open. Things were broken, including our cookie jar, but I fixed everything before Bonnie got home. I didn't want her to yell at me, thinking it was me who made the mess."

Everyone just looks at me.

They start to search again. All I do is sit on the couch next to Bonnie and watch them look around. I can't watch TV because the robbers have taken it. All Bonnie does is try Dad and Veronica repeatedly. When I look out the window, I see it is getting dark and we don't even have dinner yet, but I also see a car out front that I didn't see before. It is a dark blue car.

"That's the car!" I suddenly yell. "I saw that car when the robbers were here!"

Just then, all the officers snap their heads at me, and Officer Truman quickly goes outside to the car to check it out. The other officer, Officer Kongsberg, goes back to searching for whatever they were looking for around the house.

When I look back out the window a second time, I see Officer Truman has his gun out and is instructing the people to get out of the car. Slowly, four people get out. They are wearing all black clothes and ski masks to cover their faces. I just think, *OMG those are the robbers!*

"That's them!" I try to yell as I point, my voice shaking.

Bonnie hears me and we both look out the window to watch. After we see the four people climb out of the car dressed suspiciously, Officer Truman quickly instructs them to lean over the car with their hands behind their heads. He quickly puts them each in handcuffs and into the police car.

Once the robbers are in custody, settled in the police car, he walks up slowly to our house and comes in.

He tells us, "They won't be causing you any more trouble!"

"Oh, thank you," says Bonnie in a small quivering voice.

I am still wondering where Dad and Veronica are.

"There's just one more thing we need," I say.

"And what's that?" asks one of the officers, I am unclear which one.

"We still can't seem to contact our dad or stepmom?"

"Well I guess someone should stay here until they come home, to make sure you guys are all right. I'm just going to take these bad guys down to the station," said Officer Kongsberg.

He goes out the door, right to the car and drives away.

Officer Truman comes over and sits down on the couch beside Bonnie and me. I don't feel much like talking. I am still worried about Dad and Veronica, but mostly Dad. *They could be in trouble or maybe he's just running late? I don't know, but what are the odds that they are both late on the same day? Maybe the robbers have something to do with it? But, how could they, my Dad was at work when they came, right?*

"Lola, are you okay?" asks Bonnie.

"Of course, I'm not ok! I'm worried about Dad and Veronica, but mostly Dad, and you should be too!" I answer.

Bonnie just glances at me with sad eyes and continues to ignore me. Officer Truman continues to stare into the distance. An hour has passed, and no one has called! No Dad and no Veronica! Not even a call from the police station to ask if anything has changed. It has, so far, been quiet and awkward.

Bonnie and Officer Truman start a halfway conversation. Bonnie has just finished telling him of what she does when she goes to the clubs. By the way he's sitting on the sofa, looking bored out of his mind, it seems to me that like most of her friends, he doesn't care. I can tell the officer is getting sick and tired of waiting for my parents to finally arrive home. Tired of "babysitting" us. A couple of more hours have passed and still no answer.

At this point, we are beyond worried, both of us! We are hungry, too! Officer Truman asks us if we have any family in the neighborhood, someone we could stay with for the time being. It's getting late, and he doesn't want us to be alone for the night. He is also getting tired of staying with us and listening to Bonnie's boring conversations. I am certainly bored out of my mind, too. I also wonder where our TV and any other missing stuff went.

"When are we going to get our stuff back?" I ask.

"We're going to have to ask the robbers more questions about that, find out what they did with it," the officer says. Then he just goes back to staring again into the distance.

"If you don't mind, I'm going to get in the shower," Bonnie says while marching up the staircase.

The situation gets even more awkward with just the two of us, Officer Truman and I, both still sitting on the sofa and occasionally glancing at each other in contemplation, wondering what to do.

He gets up quickly off the sofa and blurts out, "I'll be right back," while swiftly walking to the kitchen with his phone in his hand.

I'm guessing he wants to call someone to come "babysit" for us or he's calling his family and telling them that he's going to be late. I don't know.

Suddenly, my sister's phone starts ringing. Someone is calling! She forgot it on the sofa; she was in such a hurry to get out of the room. *Maybe it's Dad or Veronica!* I quickly run over and pick up the phone, but unfortunately, the ringing stops. *Of course, it stops ringing! Oh, come on!*

I'm holding Bonnie's phone, thinking of something to do, when the officer comes back from the kitchen looking down with sad eyes. I walk over to him and tell him about the phone call. He yanks Bonnie's phone right out of my hands and immediately tries to redial that number. There's no answer, but someone did text her. There were instructions to meet them somewhere.

"I'm going to see what these jerks want," he tells me, "You and your sister stay here and lock the doors behind me. Don't leave the house! No matter what!"

I understand what he says and right after he hurries out the door, I am about to lock it when I notice him coming back inside. I have a confused look on my face.

"Umm..." he begins, searching for an explanation, "I really need to get back to the police station. Do you know anyone who has a vehicle that I can borrow?"

I am thinking. I don't at first think that I do know of any, but then I remember Veronica's old Scooter.

"There's Veronica's scooter in the garage," I tell him. "I don't know if it works but I can give you the keys."

I look over and see a very large grin on his face. Getting up from the couch, I go over near the garage door where the keys are hanging and hand him the keys.

"Thank you," he says and goes right into the garage.

Out of nowhere I hear the engine run. *Oh, it does work.* I thought it was broken. That's when I hear the garage door open.   I hurry back onto the sofa and watch him through the window disappearing down the road. Once he is gone, I return to my usual place on the sofa and think about Dad. *Is he okay? And who would run over and destroy my garden?*

Another thought suddenly enters my head, *WOW! Bonnie's taking forever in the shower, maybe I should check on her?*

Chapter 6

I walk up the steps but don't hear anything. I don't hear the water running. I don't hear Bonnie talking to herself, like she usually does. I hear nothing but silence! I walk slowly to the bathroom door, very quietly opening it. The only sound is the creaking of the old door.

"Bonnie, are you all right?" I ask.

When I open the bathroom door, I see her dressed body lying on the floor and she's not moving! I quickly run over to her and see if I can find a pulse. *Nothing! She's dead! How? What happened? Why? Who did it?*

I want, I need to get someone, to get help! The police station is probably closed. It's late and Officer Truman left. I do the only thing I can think of, I start screaming and yelling for help! But of course, no one can hear me because there's no one around. I just grab her hand and hold it tightly and put her head on my knees and just start crying. She may be like the meanest sister ever, but I still don't know what I'm going to do without her.

After I calm myself down, I spot another pregnancy test. I put her head gently back down on the floor and I let go of her hand. I pick up the pregnancy test. It says negative! *Wait, I thought she was? Maybe she had a miscarriage before she died? Or maybe she killed it? Maybe the test was mistaken? I don't know what's going on!*

First, my garden, then the robbers, then Dad and Veronica are nowhere to be found, and now this!

I thought I had a good life and nothing bad was ever going to happen. Well, maybe some little things, but not this! Now my sister is gone! I'm alone in the house, and who knows if these robbers have friends?

I happen to glance down at Bonnie's body. I see blood. I kneel and open her shirt. It looks to me like she's been shot. *How?* I didn't hear anything go off. No big bangs, or firecracker sounds, nothing like that; the house was silent.

I look around the bathroom. The thought occurs to me that maybe she wanted to kill herself. I search near and behind the toilet, nothing. I look in the sink, still nothing. I open all the cabinets and I still can't find anything. I happen to glance at the window and see a hole in the glass. *Wait a second! That's how!*

Someone shot her through the window. I still don't know what to do. Maybe I should leave her here so when the officer comes back, he can investigate and because she's too heavy for me to move. I sadly leave the bathroom closing the door behind me. I feel lost! I end up returning to my spot on the sofa.

Now I feel alone in this big house. I feel empty inside. My heart is breaking. I just give up. I thought I had this perfect life and nothing could go wrong, but I was so wrong. For the one hundredth time today, questions go swimming through my mind. *What happened to her? Who shot her? What happened to Dad and Veronica? Are the policemen coming back?*

While I wonder these things, I realize I'm heading back up the stairs, toward my room. I automatically fall down on my bed. I can't help but cry. My emotions are all over the place, uncontrollable. It has been a big, scary, extremely sad day. I'm wishing this is all a dream, a very bad dream. I realize, only now, how drained I really am. Exhaustion takes me. I close my eyes without a battle and fall into a deep sleep. Maybe tomorrow will be a better day.

The next morning, I wake up to ear piercing sirens. *Wait, is that the ambulance?* I jump out of my bed quickly and really slowly open my door, peeking out. Wherever I look I see policemen and lots of them! They are everywhere. Suddenly one of them notices me. *Hey! That's Officer Truman!* In the next instant he is walking towards me.

"I thought the robbers took you," he says jokingly. "Do you know what happened to your sister?"

While I try to explain to him what I saw, what I found last night, he has a weird look on his face. It isn't a surprised look at all.

"I know who shot your sister!"

"Who?" I ask.

"It was your mother!" he responds.

While waiting for this new information to sink in, I keep thinking, *Why would Veronica do that?*

"You're talking about Veronica, right?" I ask.

"No," says Officer Truman. "Your real mother."

My what? I thought she was dead! Officer Truman looks back at me and starts to explain that she never died. My father just said that so he could keep me safe.

"He discovered what a bad person she was and tried to protect you," the officer explains.

He goes on to say that my mother shot my sister by mistake. She thought Bonnie was Veronica. After she shot her, she realized what she had done. She ran off and stashed the gun in a nearby bush.

"The fingerprints on the gun are a match to your mother's."

I can't believe my ears. My mother's alive! She's the one who shot Bonnie!

"Is Bonnie going to be okay?" I ask.

Officer Truman bends down on his knees and looks me straight in the eyes as he continues, "I'm sorry, but she's gone."

I don't know what to think. After he tells me that, I freeze. I don't know what to do. *My sister is gone! Why did this have to happen to me?* I think I'm going into shock.

Officer Truman takes me by the hand and begins walking me down the stairs. That's when I see Veronica. I quickly run down the remainder of the steps and right into her arms, giving her a big hug. For the first time ever, I'm glad she's here.

"Bonnie is…" my voice trails off unable to find the words to explain.

"I already know what happened to her," Veronica interjects to save me.

As we look at each other sadly, we see something being carried carefully down the stairs. It's Bonnie, in a black body bag.

I can't seem to take my eyes off the black bag heading outside and into a waiting dark colored van. Veronica is crying quietly as she gently wipes away her falling tears.

While the van leaves, the police leave too.

"Well, there's no more here to investigate," says one of the policemen as he walks out the door. Officer Truman stays with us until the last officer leaves.

"We don't know where your dad is quite yet, but we will get on it asap and find him," he says when he is the only one left.

"Please find him!" begs Veronica.

"We will, that's a promise!" says Officer Truman as he leaves.

The front door closes. I turn to Veronica who is on her phone, telling someone what has happened. I'm sure it's one of her friends. I wait patiently.

"Where were you at this whole time?" I ask as she finally hangs up her phone.

She looks at me, straight into my eyes, and starts to calmly explain what she has gone through, what exactly happened to her.

"I was knocked out. I woke up and found out I was in a very dark place. I couldn't even see my fingers in front of my face. It was very hard to breathe. I felt like I was suffocating. There was no room to move. It was very tight. I could not sit up, could not turn around. I could only lie on my back. Underneath me was soft, kind of like a big pillow. It was very quiet, so quiet you could hear a pin drop. If I concentrated, I thought I heard men talking very softly, whispering really. I realized they were talking about me. I heard rustling sounds and lots of moving right above me. It sounded like it was on top of me. I didn't know what it was. I didn't know what was happening.   Suddenly, I was moving, well whatever I was in was moving. A bright blinding light quickly filled my vision. I was temporarily blinded, but I could breathe again. I took heavy breaths and coughed as the air refilled my lungs.

I was in shock once I found out the reason why I could not move or breathe. It became clear to me that my temporary coffin had been opened. I finally looked around sitting inside an actual coffin. The coffin itself was tan in color and had tan bedding I was currently sitting on. I looked around and saw dozens and dozens of fake flowers on the ground that looked to be sunflowers and roses and tulips. All the flowers we had in our once beautiful garden. Someone was trying to cover up the recent digging, the recent burial. On the other side of me I saw tons of policemen. One of them took my hand and helped lift me out of the box. After I seemed stable and able to stand, I looked around and saw that I was buried under the garden. The Officers said that I was under there for several hours. Someone had knocked me out and buried me under there, left me to die. I could have, and probably would have died, but fortunately the officers found me in time."

"Do you know who put you under there?" I ask in bewilderment.

"The Officers say it was robbers, but the leader of the robbers told them to do it. They found out the leader is actually your mother."

I couldn't believe my ears. How could my mother do all of that? I get up from the couch and head out back, where the garden is - or was. I look out and can't believe what I see. An open casket sits on the torn up ground - an actual real coffin. Fake flowers are scattered all over the ground. Everything looks dug up and ruined. How could she do this?

I go back inside and sit down next to Veronica.

"I'm going to bed, I'm so tired," says Veronica. "Don't stay up too late, okay?"

She walks up to her room and I hear the door close. I just sit here. *Alone. Again.* I don't know what to do. I am thinking of how I can find my dad and why my mother would do this. I thought she loved us.

As I think of how terrible my day was, I decide it is the worst day ever! *The worst day of my life!* I slowly drag myself up the stairs and into my room. I close my door behind me and slowly stroll over to my bed. My mind is whirling. I lie down and think about Veronica and what she has gone through.

As I close my eyes, I picture what my mother looked like before, as I remember her when I was little. Dark brown hair, blue eyes, she always smelled like lilacs. I think of how she was so nice to us and how much she loved us. *Where did she go if she didn't die? Did she try to find us? What did she do back then that my father had to protect us from?*

Again, the questions come rushing. *Why would she shoot my sister? What has she been doing all these years? Why, why, why...* So many questions to which I will probably never know the answers. I know the assumed why for some of my questions because of what Officer Truman told me, but it's so hard to believe! *What could have changed in her mind, in her life to be so drastic? What was she thinking?*

I missed her terribly when I thought she had died, but now I never want to see her ever again. I hate her for what she's done. Without realizing how tired I've become, I doze off to sleep.

Chapter 7

The next morning, I hear a lot of noise in the bathroom. I get up from my bed and head in that direction. I see Veronica cleaning up Bonnie's blood off the bathroom floor. I see her scrubbing and crying at the same time. *Of course, the officers didn't help clean that up yesterday.* I see her scrubbing hard with bleach and cleaner. It's gradually coming off, but she's really scrubbing. I want to say something, but I don't know what to say, so I look for something else to do instead.

In my pajamas, I head outside to get the mail that wasn't brought in yesterday. When I open the mailbox, I see a lot of bills, but then I see a letter. It's addressed to Veronica! That's weird; she never gets mail except for her hair or nail appointment reminders. Even though it's Veronica's letter, I open it up and I read it as I walk into the house. It says:

Dear Veronica,

This is Ella, Lola's real mother. If you don't come to 555 East Street Lane after sunset tomorrow night at 8pm. I am going to kill your husband. If you do come, you have to stay, but he will be able to leave. It's one or the other, or I will kill you both. Do not tell the police or I will be forced to kill your whole family.

Sincerely,

Ella

OMG! I have to tell Veronica. If she goes, I will get my dad back, but Veronica will die. I can't tell the police, or my mother will kill all of us. I don't know what to do.

As I walk upstairs to tell Veronica, I see that she's not in the bathroom anymore. I walk over to her bedroom with the letter in my hand and open the door. I see her lying down on her bed; I think she's asleep. Then, I hear her loud snores. *Okay, yes, she is asleep. That's good.*

I walk out into the hallway and close the door softly behind me. I don't want to wake her up. I'm aware that she had a long horrible day. I am wracking my brain for what to do, and I have a thought. *What if I call the police and tell them what happened, but then go into hiding right after, so if my mother finds out the police were called, she won't know where I went?* She wouldn't be able to find me.

I open Veronica's bedroom door slowly. I see her role over. *Oh no, did I wake her?* Then, I suddenly hear her snore again. *Okay, good, she's still out.* I spot her pink sparkly phone sitting on her bedside table and walk slowly toward it. The floorboards squeak beneath my feet. I quickly grab her phone and run out of her room closing the door behind me. I turn on her phone and there is a password. *Of course, there is.*

I am thinking of what this password could be. It can't be her birthday because the numbers aren't long enough. Besides, I don't know when her birthday is anyway. I try the combination for the safe that's in my dad's room. *Oh my gosh, it works! Wow, how creative, Veronica.* Then, I dial the numbers 911. It starts to ring.

The operator answers, "911 What is your emergency?"

And this is where I freeze. I don't know what to say. I have never talked to the police on the phone before. After a frustrating pause, I find my voice and start to tell them about what happened to Bonnie and about the letter.

They don't answer right away. Then, they suddenly say they're on their way. I don't know if that means to my house or to the address that I have given them from the letter. They end the call and I put the phone down.

That's when I hear Veronica call my name from the bedroom. I open the door and head inside. She has a questionable look on her face, probably wondering why I have her phone in my hand. I look over at her, handing her the letter. I tell her that I have called the police and suggest that we hide somewhere so my mother cannot find us.

After she reads the letter, Veronica just stares at me with teary eyes. I'm guessing she's in shock from the letter. A few seconds pass that seem like minutes. I can tell she is thinking about something. She suddenly mentions that maybe it was a good idea that I called the police after all.

Not knowing what to do next, Veronica asks me if I would mind helping her curl and style her hair. Apparently, lying in the coffin had flattened it. That's just like her to want to look her best with nowhere to go. I agree, hoping to take our minds off things. It isn't long until we hear the front doorbell.

We look at each other in surprise and quickly but quietly go downstairs. We don't know who it is. *Is it the police again, or is it my mother here to finish what she started?*

We secretly peek out the corner of the window and find a policeman waiting outside. With me standing right behind her, Veronica opens the door.

"It's Officer Truman! It's okay. I know him," I say, turning to Veronica.

He starts to speak, "We found your dad. He was captured by your mother. Thanks to your call, we arrested your mother and her 'pals' just in time. Your father is all right. He is currently at the hospital getting checked out. I can take you there if you want. Also, Bonnie's body is ready to be transferred into your custody. The funeral home is waiting for you to call them to make the funeral arrangements."

I can't believe my ears! My dad is all right! This is the best news. I'm so glad that we are now safe! I turn to Veronica who is currently hugging the policeman.

"Thank you so much. And yes, we would appreciate a ride," says Veronica.

The officer looks down at her and says courteously, "Just doing my job, Ma'am."

We follow him to the police car. Veronica and I climb in the back. It is a quiet, but happy ride. When we arrive at the hospital, Officer Truman gets out first and opens the door for us.

We both get out and say, "Thank you," in appreciation.

While walking into the hospital, Officer Truman is informing us that Veronica and my dad were not my mother's only targets. She was also going after other people, but they have no idea why. He continues to say that when they found my dad, there were five other people that were captured there as well. He says that jail is not the right place for her. They dropped her off at a mental asylum.

I just cannot believe that she would do any of this! I can't believe that anyone could do these things, really. *It's good that they are getting her help*, I think.

"Thank you for everything," says Veronica with tears in her eyes.

Then we walk inside. The hospital is really busy. It is packed; there are very few open chairs. I notice people crying, people talking, babies crying, and a few old people who have fallen asleep. I can only imagine the problems they are all facing.

Officer Truman looks at us and tells us to sit down and he will be right back. It is hard to find a seat right next to each other. We eventually find three seats together and grab them. While we sit down, he walks up to the receptionist at the nurse's station. I hear them talking but their voices are whispers.

I glance over to Veronica who is at the vending machine getting a snack. She eats when she's stressed. Then, I see a cookie drop down from the vending machine. She picks it out and opens the wrapper really fast. I think she must be really stressed because she never eats sweets. Generally, she doesn't get that stressed out. The last time she was really stressed out is when the hairdresser messed up her hair cut. I watch her take a big monster size bite out of the cookie. *Geez!*

Officer Truman comes over and tells us that my dad is okay, and we can see him shortly. I am so happy he is all right! I don't know what I would do if he wasn't. I mean, *Living by myself with Veronica? That would be a disaster!*

Twenty minutes have passed, and I look over at Officer Truman who is asleep. He had a long day. *How can he be asleep though? It's so noisy and loud here.* Then I look over to where Veronica was sitting, but she's not sitting there anymore. I see her at the vending machine again, but this time she's asleep on the floor with half of a cookie sticking out of her mouth. There's a lot of wrappers around her. *It's going to take a while to burn those calories away*, I think.

Then this lady comes to us and says, "Excuse me, your father can have visitors now," while looking at me.

"Okay," I say while I try to wake up Officer Truman. He eventually wakes up and I tell him that we can go see my dad now.

We stand up and he asks, "What about Veronica?"

"We will get her later. She had a long day," I say quietly.

Chapter 8

We walk out of the noisy waiting room and head into an elevator. We don't say much except for when Officer Truman tells me what number to push.

When the elevator doors open, a lady steps on while we step off. She looks familiar, but I don't know why.

We walk down the creepy hallway and head into Dad's room. I don't know his room number, so Officer Truman leads the way.

"It's right here," he points to a sign by the door that reads Room 56. "I'll wait out here," says Officer Truman as he sits down on a chair in the hallway.

As I walk in his room, I keep thinking about what happened and what will happen if my mom escapes. *What if she tries to go back to my dad again?* I close the door quietly behind me, just in case he's sleeping. Then, I hear a TV. I think it's the news. *He is awake!*

As I walk over to him really quietly, I hear him say, "Yes? Is someone there?"

I don't know why I'm nervous. I push over a privacy curtain that is hanging on the ceiling and say, "Hey, Daddy."

He looks at me with his bright glossy blue eyes. He starts to tear up and opens his arms for a hug. I run to him and give him the biggest hug in the world.

"Where's Veronica and Bonnie?" I hear him ask.

"Well, Veronica is downstairs asleep in the waiting room because she was stress eating and fell asleep," I say.

He just laughs. "Of course, she is," he giggles. I've missed his laugh. As I start to explain where Bonnie is, Veronica comes in.

She looks at him with a giant smile on her face and hugs him. She also gives him a big sloppy kiss which is gross, so I have to look away.

Then, he asks again, "So where is Bonnie?"

We both look at each other with sad eyes, trying to figure out what to say. We don't want to tell him or we both are going to cry, but I know that we must.

I try to explain, "So when you got captured Bonnie was taking a shower while I was downstairs. And- well -she-um-she- she-got shot," I shudder, blurting it out. "I swear I didn't hear any gunshots. When I went up to check on her, she was lying on the floor. I just thought she fainted, but then I saw the blood..."

At this time, I know he is crying. Then I begin to tell the rest of the story. "It looked like a gunshot to me so I was looking around for a gun or something and I couldn't find anything."

He interrupts me saying, "Who did it, Lola?"

I am thinking of what to say. I am scared. I begin to reveal what we know, "It was my mother. She shot through the bathroom window. The cops said she thought Bonnie was Veronica."

My dad has a huge confused look on his face, obviously in shock. He just turns his head and stares into the distance. I don't think he knows what to say.

Finally, he begins to say something as Veronica sits down crying, "I thought she was with me?"

Veronica starts to talk with weeping words, "When the cops found you, you were knocked out. Maybe after you fainted, she left and went to our house."

After a bit of silence Officer Truman steps in.

"Who are you?" asks my dad.

"I'm Officer Truman. I helped your family for a while. I kept them safe and I watched out for them and I helped find you," says Officer Truman.

"Thank you for all your help and for keeping Lola and Veronica safe," says my dad as he gives Officer Truman a handshake.

"Well we should give your dad some rest. Let's go to the waiting room, you guys," says Veronica as she's standing up from the chair.

As we are walking out, I wave him goodbye and say, "Get some rest. We will see you later."

We walk out with Officer Truman in the lead and me closing the door quietly behind us. As we head to the elevator, I keep thinking, *If he's really all right, when will he be able to go home*? I am also wondering how Veronica is doing with all this. *Is she all right? She should be glad I'm worrying about her because I never do*. I'm also wondering why Officer Truman is still here. *Doesn't he have a family he needs to go to?*

We walk into the elevator and I push the bottom floor button. It is quiet in the elevator. Awkward quiet. As the elevator doors open, we walk out and pass the vending machine that Veronica was at earlier. Her wrappers are still all over the floor. *Of course, she didn't pick them up. She's so messy.*

While we find a seat, Veronica goes over and picks up all the wrappers around the vending machines. She must feel better that she's cleaning up her mess.

As we sit, I want to ask Officer Truman about if he should go home to his family. So that's what I do, "Thank you for all your help, but you can leave and go home to your family."

He just looks away in sadness, then turns back to say, "I don't have anyone to go to. I live alone. I have nowhere to go. This is all I do is my job."

I don't know what to say. I feel bad for him. *Maybe he can live with us?* We need extra protection because of what happened today. As I think of how I should ask Veronica if he can stay with us, I see my dad coming out of the elevator and down the hall with a nurse helping him.

I get up from my seat in a hurry to go see him again. As I am running over, I must startle Veronica because she jumps awake from sleep. Then, she starts to walk towards him too.

As we get to him the nurse says, "He's all yours! He can go home now. Just make sure he gets enough sleep and takes his medication."

"Thank you," says Veronica.

We help walk him to the counter to check out. As Veronica is signing the papers dad looks over to me with a nice calming grin. I think he may have taken too many meds because he never smiles at me like that. I begin to laugh in my head.

While we walk outside Officer Truman asks if he can stay at our house for a while to make sure everything is safe for us.

"Well, sure you can," says Dad, "We would be happy to have you."

"Oh, and by the way, do you guys need a ride home?" asks Officer Truman.

"We would love that," says Veronica happily.

When we get in the car, I feel safe. I haven't felt safe for a while and having my dad back, I don't feel alone anymore. I'm glad I get to sit next to my dad in the back seat while Veronica sits up front.

As we drive, I look out the window and stare at the bright moon looking back at me. I am also looking at the bright beautiful stars all over the dark night sky. There's hope.

Chapter 9

It isn't long before we are home. When we get home all the lights are still on, but that's okay because we were in a rush to see my dad. Dad and I scooch out of the police car and head to the porch.

"If it's all right with you, I need to go to the police station to fill out today's reports and go get an overnight bag from my house," says Officer Truman.

"That is all right," says Veronica, "I will put some blankets and pillows in the guest room for you."

"Thank you," says Officer Truman as he heads out the door.

As we head inside, we all sit on the sofa. I don't think any of us are tired. Dad reaches for the end table grabbing the remote. He is about to push the power button, when he notices the TV is gone.

"What happened to the TV?" asks Dad.

I look over at him and explain, "When I got home from school yesterday, I went out to the flower garden to water them, and when I came back in the whole house was trashed. There were cabinets and drawers open. The TV was gone, and the kitchen chairs were all over the place."

He doesn't look surprised. "Yes, that's right, there were robbers. Did they take anything out of the safe in my closet?" Dad asks.

"No, they didn't make it upstairs," I answer.

He has a faraway stare as if thinking. "That's good," he adds shortly.

I'm surprised he's not asking me more questions. Then out of nowhere, Dad gets up and says, "I'm going to bed to read."

He walks to the bookshelf to find a book. Then, holding a book in one hand and his phone in the other, he heads upstairs. A few seconds later I hear his bedroom door close. I guess Veronica thinks that is a good idea because she herself now walks to the bookshelf and gets a book called *How To Be Like Royalty*. She likes those kinds of books because she likes their lifestyle. She brings her book and sits back down back on the couch, pulling a blanket over her lap and getting comfortable.

I don't want to read, but I am a little hungry. I get up from the couch and head into the kitchen. I get out the supplies to make a peanut butter jelly sandwich. When I finish making my sandwich, I put everything away and head outside to the flower garden. Surprisingly, I'm not that cold out here.

Outside, I see the dark of night and the only lights are the back-porch light and the bright moon looking down on me. The only sounds are an owl hooting and the crickets chirping. Then I notice the moonlight hitting the edge of the coffin. It's still here from when Veronica was in it underground.

People must think we're strange having a coffin in our backyard. Others have no idea what has happened recently to our family. *Good thing we don't have any neighbors!* I'd hate to think what would go through their minds.

I have a sudden thought, *That would be a good place for me to sit and eat my sandwich while looking back at the moon!* I'm not going to close it, that would be crazy. I head over to the coffin and crisscross my legs inside. I take my first bite of my sandwich and listen to the calming sounds of nature around me. After I finish my sandwich for some reason, I lie back in the coffin. I rest my head on the soft pillow and look back at the stars and the moon above, sparkling at me. Before I realize it, I'm slowly closing my eyes.

Chapter 10

The next few days pass like a blur. I don't go to school because of what happened, and my dad doesn't care that I miss. I don't hang out with my friends or do much of anything. I just stay quiet in my room, until today. Today, I don't have much choice. I must part from the security of my room. Today is Bonnie's funeral.

When I get up from my warm bed, I head to the bathroom still in my Hello Kitty pajamas. I think everyone else is still sleeping because there is no noise in the house, no one is up yet. I take my time in the bathroom, not feeling rushed.

Coming back through the bathroom doorway, Veronica is standing in the hallway waiting for me. She has a very depressing look. She gently pushes past me and closes the door behind her. That's odd. She usually yells at me because apparently, I always take too long. Well, I'm sure she is sad about today, just like everyone else, so maybe that's why she is acting this way.

As I head back into my room, I hear something downstairs. *Is that bacon I smell, and coffee?* I think someone is cooking breakfast. I will go down after I get dressed.

In my room I close my door quietly behind me, just in case my dad is still sleeping. I pick out my outfit. It's a long black dress with small flowers on it. After some consideration, I put my emerald necklace, that my mom gave me, back into my jewelry box. It suddenly doesn't mean the same to me now as it did before. I pick out my pearl one instead. I also add a black headband to complete the outfit that matches the dress. I really like this dress, but not for funerals.

My mother's funeral suddenly comes to mind. It is still sad even though she wasn't really dead. The feelings were real. It's hard to believe she was still alive at that time.

As I open my bedroom door to head downstairs, I see Veronica coming out of the bathroom. She looks quite depressed and sad. This is the quietest she's ever been. I continue downstairs to the kitchen. I put my shoes, phone, and jacket on the counter and see scrambled eggs in a frying pan on the stove. I don't see anyone in the kitchen.

Who is awake? I think.

Then, I see someone coming from the garage door. It's Officer Truman coming in from getting vegetables for the eggs. I almost forgot he was here.

"Morning," he says as he chops up the vegetables.

"Hi," I whisper.

After all the vegetables are chopped, he places them with the eggs in the frying pan and stirs them together. As I watch him cook, I hear Dad's bedroom door open and hear him walk down the steps.

"That smells good! Thank you!" Dad says while opening the fridge and getting out the orange juice. I didn't even know we had orange juice.

Officer Truman opens the cabinets with the plates and starts setting the table. He knows where everything is like he's been here before.

"You guys are so nice for letting me stay here, so I thought I should cook breakfast for everyone," says Officer Truman as he slides the eggs onto the plates.

"That's so kind and you're welcome," says dad as he pats Officer Truman on the back.

I like having Officer Truman here. He's like an uncle to me now. I guess that happens when you go through something traumatic together.

I grab my plate of eggs and my cup of orange juice and head to the table. Officer Truman turns off the stove and grabs his plate and heads to the table too. My dad is already waiting at the table eating. *Where Is Veronica?* I thought she was awake.

With just a few pieces of egg left on my plate, I finally see Veronica coming down the stairs in a long plain black dress with a black checkered design shawl and a pair of black high heels that make her look. Those heels make her taller than my dad. She walks to the kitchen and takes her plate, and a cup of coffee and sits down next to Dad, not saying a word. She usually talks a lot, so much it usually gets annoying. It's weird not hearing her talk at all. I notice, as she chews her food, she takes the smallest bites possible. Seems like she doesn't have much of an appetite.

I get up from the table and put my dishes in the sink. Then I go over and sit on the recliner next to the sofa in the living room. It's usually Dad's chair and he doesn't let anyone sit here, but I guess he doesn't care today. It's quiet in the house this morning. No one has said much since we woke up. The only person not dressed at this point is Officer Truman. I think it's because he's been busy cooking breakfast.

Just as I notice him still in his pajamas, he suddenly gets up, puts his dishes in the sink, and heads upstairs. It's like he read my mind. I'm guessing he's going up to get dressed.

As I sit patiently on the chair, Dad takes both Veronica's and his dishes and puts them in the sink. I think dad was waiting for Veronica to finish her food. He sits back down next to Veronica who is now looking at her phone. She's probably looking at Facebook to see who's coming to the funeral.

I look up at the stairs and see Officer Truman coming down. He's wearing a suit just like my dad. It's weird seeing him not in his police uniform. Then Dad gets up and grabs his phone and keys from the small table beside the front door. Well, I guess he's ready to leave. We all get up and follow behind him. The dishes will wait till we get back, I guess.

Dad waits to be last out the door and locks it behind us. On our way to the car, it starts to drizzle, the cold drops hitting our faces. *Of course, it has to rain today.* Officer Truman offers to drive us. Dad sits beside him up front. I have to sit next to Veronica in the back. She has on way too much perfume. I'm sure it will smell up the whole car.

As we drive down the road I kind of feel weird for being in a police car. Before it was fun, but now it's weird. I notice if people look at us, they may think that we did something wrong. As we drive along, I look out my window imagining how this is going to go. I haven't heard if it's going to be an open casket or closed. I don't want it to be an open casket. I really don't want to see her like that.

The drive is over before we know it. We are pulling up the driveway to the funeral home. It looks kind of like a church. We park right next to a silver van. I think my grandma drives that. I haven't seen her in a while because she doesn't get along with Veronica, which no one ever has except for my dad and Bonnie.

As we make our way inside, I see a large staircase right inside the entryway that heads upstairs. A sign says, "Do not trespass." Apparently, that's only for the people that work here. Instead, we head down a tannish hallway. There are two doors propped open at the end awaiting our arrival. When we get close to the doors there is a signup sheet on a small table, like a guest book. It appears to be for everyone who comes to sign.

"You guys head inside and find a seat," says Dad as he's grabbing a pen to sign the guest book.

As we head inside the two open doors, we find our seats in the front. Ours are reserved. We are some of the first few people here. I start to look around. There are windows on both sides of the room with a giant chandelier on the ceiling. Each seat is covered with a red seat cover. It's really pretty.

My gaze turns to the front of the room. I hear more people coming in, but I pay no attention. It's hard to miss Bonnie's light pink casket. It kind of looks like the one in the backyard. I notice it's closed and has a ton of sunflowers on the top, which were her favorite. It's good that it's closed, because I really don't know if I could stand it being open.

When it seems that everyone has come, a man starts walking up to the front next to Bonnie with a microphone and announces his name and starts talking. He seems to be the director, but I'm really not sure since I've not been paying much attention. While he's speaking, I look around and see who's here.

I see my aunts, uncles, cousins, grandparents, and even my best friend is here sitting behind us. I didn't even notice them come in. I also see some people I don't know. In the same row, on the other side of the aisle is a boy that looks about Bonnie's age, crying. *Wow, I've never seen a man cry.*

When my gaze looks up at the man who's still talking, I notice he's talking about how great Bonnie was and that she will always be missed. I don't want to cry, but tears are starting to flow down my face. At least I'm not the only one crying. I look over at Veronica who is crying so much that her face is tomato red with several used tissues on her lap.

I try not to listen to the man talking because I know it will make things worse. He finishes talking and asks my dad if he wants to come up and say a few words. I don't think my dad wants to go, because it takes him longer to walk up there than usual.

He reaches the microphone and starts to talk, "Well-um-I didn't know I had to come up here or I would have written something down," he says. The crowd of people smile.

He stops for a second and thinks of what to say next.

He starts to speak again, "Bonnie was a good kid. Ever since she was little, she always loved sunflowers," as he points to the sunflowers on top of her casket. "One time she made me park on the side of a highway so she could get out and get some flowers that were there. She helped plant those flowers in the flower garden we have. Of course, they died because she forgot to water them." The crowd starts to laugh.

"When she was just a toddler, she used to have a sunflower blanket she would carry around with her wherever she went. When she would forget where she put that thing, it was like it was the end of the world for her. Some of you may know her as 'Bonnie the party girl' because ever since she moved here, she was always going to parties and stuff, but I will always remember her as 'Bonnie the Sunflower girl'."

He hands the microphone to one of Bonnie's friends who is speaking next. As he sits down, I can tell that that was very hard for him to do. He has tears in his eyes.

Bonnie's friend speaks, "Hi, I'm Bonnie's best friend, Sierra. Ever since she moved here, she was a sister to me. She was the closest thing I had to one. We've known each other since we were five and were always best friends. She never told me that she likes sunflowers, but I should have known. She is just like one.

She's different, she's fun, and loving and beautiful. I just can't believe she's gone. When we were little, we had a silly agreement that whoever dies first has to haunt the other one for life, which I thought was just a silly game at the time, but now I don't want her to haunt me." The crowd giggles. "I want her to make it to heaven and have a fun and a happy life up there. Thank you, my sister," she says in a sad quiet voice.

She hands the microphone back to the director and he starts talking more about her. I don't really listen anymore. I just want this to be over. About twenty minutes pass and he asks us, if we want, to come up to the casket to say our goodbyes.

I know that I should, but I just can't. It's just too hard.

Veronica and my dad go up, holding hands, as they touch the top of the casket with their free hands. A line starts down the aisle. Each person waits to pay their respects.

As the line gets shorter and people are heading out the door, I see Officer Truman outside waiting. I head out there with him. As we stand outside, several people walk by us visibly trying to stop their tears. I also see a group of people I don't know waiting outside, too. I happen to look behind me and see Veronica and my dad walking down the hallway towards us.

When they reach us, we all head to the car. Officer Truman is again driving, and I take the back seat next to Veronica. They will be lowering Bonnie underground after everyone leaves. We are choosing not to watch that part. I think the tombstone freaks Veronica out.

As we head home, I think about this day and how it will be tomorrow. *How lonely will my life now be?* I know I didn't always get along with Bonnie, but I know I will miss her deeply. Bonnie is in a better place now. Today was sad, very sad, but it will get better as time goes on. That's what everyone says anyway.

Tomorrow will be another day.

About The Author

Makenzie R. Casseday has a creative, funny, caring personality. She has had adventures in a variety of hobbies, but art, theatre, and writing stories are her favorite!

Makenzie grew up writing short stories. Often, as a child, she would write down ideas in a notebook she carried around in her bookbag. Thrilled to be publishing her first title, she hopes that you will enjoy reading this story as much as she enjoyed writing it!

Makenzie has a strong love of all animals and hopes to work with them professionally someday. A high school graduating senior of 2020, she is excited to see what else this life holds for her! She currently lives with her mother, Jessica, younger sister, Chloe, her pet turtle, Turbo, and her mini dachshund, Scooby Doo, in Pennsylvania.

www.ingramcontent.com/pod-product-compliance
Lightning Source LLC
Chambersburg PA
CBHW070504130626
46555CB00003B/1148